Car Key Elves

By T. H. Hunter

Illustrated by Olga Gavrilovskiy

a
Tetoca Press
Release
2008

Car Key Elves

Todd H. Hunter, Inc.
PO Box 337
Puyallup, WA 98371
www.tetocapress.net
tetoca@tetocapress.net

ISBN#: 978-0-9788085-1-8

Printed by Tetoca Press
Printed in China
First Printing May 2008

Dedicated to:

My wife Barbara Hunter

and

My mother Dorothy Hunter

Who have tried to teach me to pick up after myself.

Tetoca Press pledges to publish family oriented books that are fun to read and keep from one generation to another. For other available titles: www.tetocapress.net

"Daddy, have you seen my watch?" asked five year old Ryan.

"No I haven't Son. Where did you leave it?"

"Right here! I left it right here, and now it is gone."

"If you had left it there, it should be there," said Mommy. "Gosh Ryan, you are always misplacing things," she continued.

"No I'm not! I left it right here."

"Well, it must be those Car Key Elves again," observed Daddy.

"Car Key Elves? What are car key elves?" asked Ryan.

"Yes, what are they?" asked big brother Casey.

"I'll bet they're elves that hide things," answered seven year old Theresa.

"You are right," confirmed Daddy. "They hide car keys and other small objects like watches and battery chargers."

"Daddy, tell us more about car key elves," said Theresa.

"Okay," said Daddy. "I'll tell the Car Key Elf story."

"Mind if I listen too?" asked Mommy.

"Not at all dear."

"This should be another interesting story," said Mommy.

"It all started when Elf management decided to solve the problems of unemployed elves and untidy children and adults."

"Why were the elves unemployed, Daddy?" asked Theresa.

"Well, they were part-timers and Christmas temps. Many were mischievous and liked to play jokes so they were usually the first released and last rehired."

Daddy Continued. "Elves have families too. Even mischievous elves are proud and like to work. Without work they are unhappy."

To help address the problems of messy people and unemployed, mischievous elves, management decided to hire elves to enter homes to move and hide items that were not properly hung up or stored.

This proposal was presented to the unemployed elves. They were delighted with the idea and chartered a union which they proudly called "Car Key Elf Guild".

The plan was announced to all the elves. The Guild president and other officers were officially elected.

Together the Guild officers and Elf management voted on rules for the Car Key Elf Guild Rule Book. Everything was the elf way: Efficient and proper.

After much noise and heated discussion, the rules for when to hide objects were ratified by the guild members.

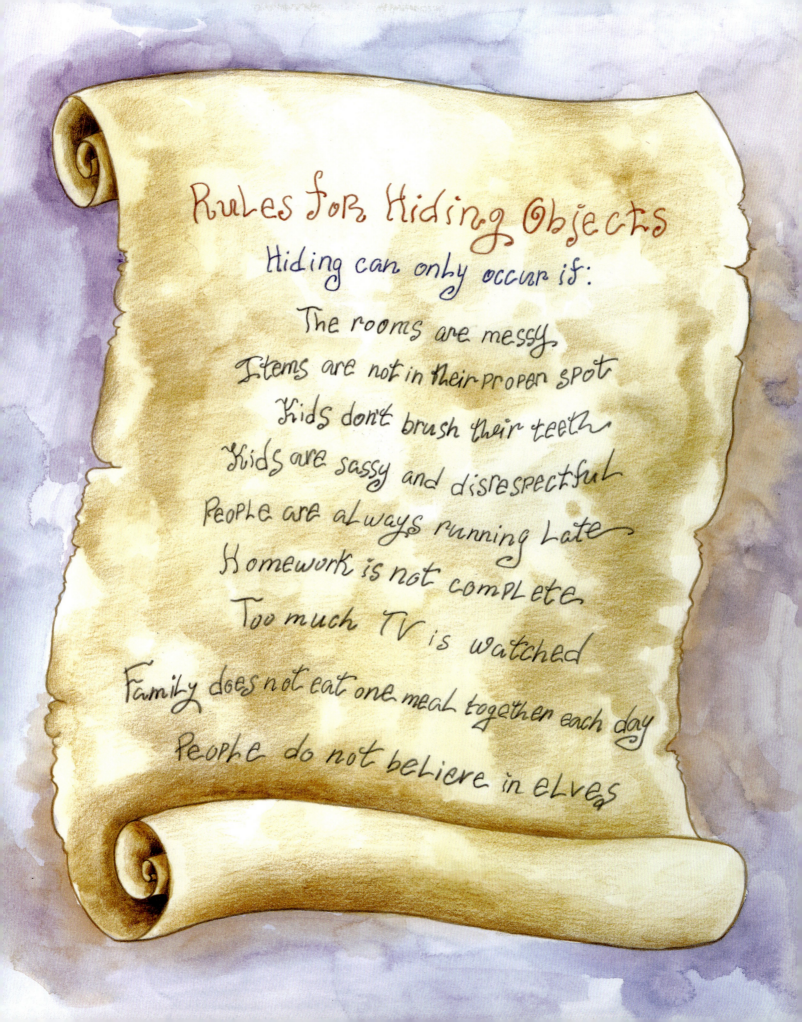

Rules for Hiding Objects

Hiding can only occur if:

The rooms are messy,

Items are not in their proper spot

Kids don't brush their teeth

Kids are sassy and disrespectful

People are always running Late

Homework is not complete

Too much TV is watched

Family does not eat one meal together each day

People do not believe in elves

At a ceremony, the rules were read to the Guild members and an oath was taken to observe them.

Meanwhile, Diginess, a loner elf, was working on her new invention when she heard about the new Car Key Elf Guild. She had not been invited to participate because she was considered too mischievous to join the Guild.

Diginess was a highly skilled, industrious worker, however her mischievous nature left her unemployed most of the time.

When employed, her mischievous sense of humor caused her
bosses problems. She would even play tricks on her fellow workers.
Rumor had it, she was part imp.

Diginess liked to fish. She created a fish lure that caught lots of fish.
She gave the fish to needy elves and their families. She had a good heart,
even if mischievous.

When she was young, a teacher unjustly blamed her for talking. She wouldn't tell on the talker so she had to sit in the corner. She was not a snitch.

So that Friday, she brought some fish and put them inside the class-
room's heater duct. There they stayed the whole week end, festering away:
Getting, smellier and smellier.

On Monday, school was cancelled for the day. The whole school had to be aired out. The kids were happy and they whispered that it must have been Diginess's work, but it couldn't be proven.

Part imp or not, Diginess was very smart and talented in the sciences, especially physics. She liked to experiment with the fourth dimension, the dimension of time. She thought her new time machine invention, named the "Hidey Hole" could be of use to the Guild.

Diginess petitioned the Guild's management, so she could demonstrate the use of the Hidey Hole to them.

The Guild's council invited Diginess to demonstrate the Hidey Hole. When summoned, she entered the demonstration room carrying a small package and requested the head elf to lend her his sled keys. With some hesitation, she received the keys.

She opened the package which contained the shimmering, transparent Hidey Hole.

"Okay now watch closely," instructed Diginess. She placed the keys in the box, tinkered with something on its side, and set the box on the table.

There was a poof of fairy dust and the box and keys were gone.

"Where are my keys?" demanded the Head Elf. "I need my sled keys."

"Don't worry, they will be back in five minutes," assured Diginess.

"Five minutes? Why five minutes?"

"I set the box to go five minutes into the future," she answered.

There was a lot of chatter as they waited. On time, the keys reappeared.
Only this time without the box, nor fairy dust.

"The box dissolves without a trace," said Diginess.

"This Hidey Hole device," said the head elf, "should only be used sparingly. Only on really messy people: Diginess."

"Yes sir."

"Looks like you now have a full-time job. Just behave yourself."

"I promise," she assured the head elf.

"So that's why I find something, after looking for it in the same place two or three times," said Mommy.

"Car Key Elves and Hidey Holes are the only explanations that make sense to me," said Daddy. "However kids, to keep the Car Key Elves away, always remember to be neat and put thing where they belong."

"Yes kids," said Mommy, "and that means Daddy too. Right Honey?"

"Yes, Honey."

The End